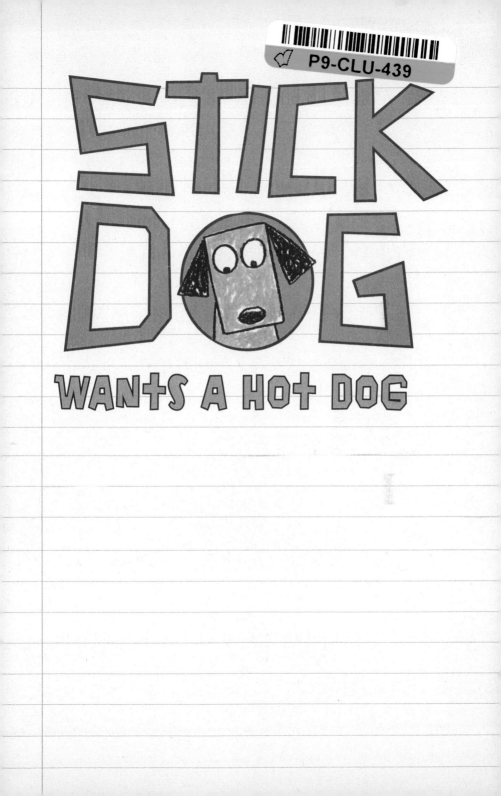

STICK DOG

WANTS A HOT DOG

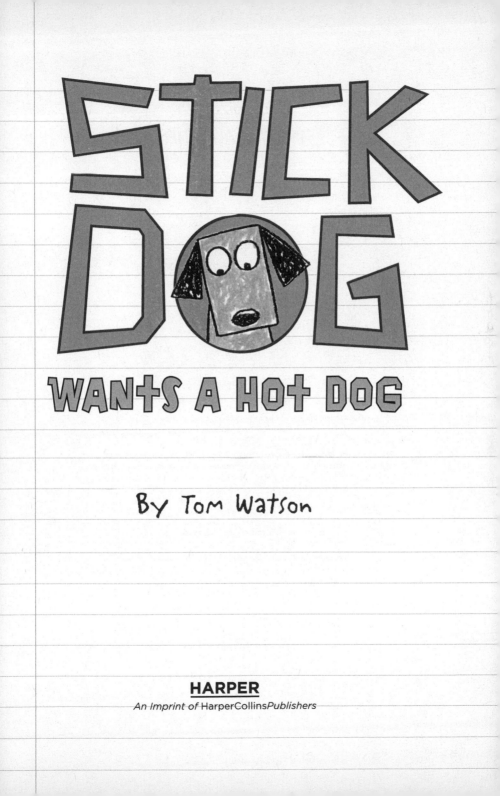

STICK DOG

WANTS A HOT DOG

By Tom Watson

HARPER
An Imprint of HarperCollinsPublishers

For Elizabeth
(YLITMDALCUTIFN)

Stick Dog Wants a Hot Dog

Copyright © 2013 by Tom Watson

Illustrations by Ethan Long based on original sketches by Tom Watson

www.harpercollinschildrens.com

Library of Congress Cataloging-in-Publication Data is available.
ISBN 978-0-06-211080-0 (trade bdg.) — ISBN 978-0-06-230450-6 (international edition)
ISBN 978-0-06-229593-4 (Scholastic edition)

Typography by Tom Starace
13 14 15 16 17   CG/BV   10 9 8 7 6 5 4 3 2 1
❖
First Edition

TABLE OF CONTENTS

Chapter 1

LET'S GET A FEW THINGS OUT OF THE WAY

This is Stick Dog.

Now, I don't really want to get into a big explanation about Stick Dog's name. See, his name is not really about HIM. It's about ME. When people aren't such good drawers, they draw stick people. Well, I draw stick dogs because I stink at drawing.

So his name is Stick Dog.

Stick Dog has four main friends—you probably met them in the first book. Their names are Mutt, Poo-Poo, Stripes, and Karen.

POO-POO

KAREN

MUTT

STRIPES

Here's some quick background on Stick
Dog's four friends.

Karen is a dachshund who loves potato
chips and once lived in the back of a
French-Asian fusion restaurant.

Mutt is a mutt. He once lived far away with
a mailman named Gary. Mutt sometimes
stores—or loses—things in his fur.

Poo-Poo is a poodle and is *not* named
after, you know, going to the bathroom.
Poo-Poo really doesn't like squirrels. Really.
A lot.

Stripes is a Dalmatian who once was a
guard dog at the mall down Highway 16.
She lost her job after the Nacho Cheese
Grande incident. She is unwilling to talk
about it.

All five dogs are strays.

It's not sad. They have each other.

The other thing you would know from the first book—besides that I don't know how to draw so well and Stick Dog has four strangely named friends—is that Stick Dog's main focus in life is food. He's always trying to find something to eat.

See, he doesn't trust humans all that much. He thinks they're kind of weird looking. If you really think about it, humans are kind of strange. I mean, why legs? How about wheels instead? And ten fingers? How about twenty? And two elbows on each arm would be better, wouldn't it? Then you could reach more places and pick up more things. And TWO eyes on ONE side of your head? How about ONE eye that spins around on top? Soooo much better, don't you think? And ears ... don't even get me started on ears.

So Stick Dog doesn't like humans because they're weird looking. But he doesn't like them for another reason too: they keep all the good food for themselves. They're a bunch of no-good, sneaky, food-hogging, only-have-fur-on-top-of-their-heads, keep-everything-for-themselves evil beasts. This one family did give them some food once at Picasso Park (well, the dogs actually sort of earned the food with this great plan that sort of worked and sort of didn't). They gave them hamburgers ... but that was really just kind of a miracle thing. That was in the first book.

Okay, Stick Dog basics: bad drawing by me, Stick Dog's friends have weird names, finding food really important, can't trust humans. Good enough?

Great.

Oh, wait, one more thing before we get started. The fact that I'm not such a good drawer is something that I accept and live with. But I sort of need you to accept and live with it too. In other words, you and I need to agree that you won't interrupt me when the drawings are not so good.

For instance, if I'm in the middle of describing a UFO that has landed right in front of Stick Dog, you're not allowed to interrupt and say something like,

"Excuse me, but that UFO looks more like the pancake I had for breakfast than a spaceship full of aliens."

UFO ↑

PANCAKE ↑

We agree that this will be a hassle-free experience, right?

Also, I tend to get distracted and sometimes go off on little side stories now and then. Or I might, for instance, stop and provide some small bit of wisdom or make a little comment. It's just who I am. I can't help it. You'll need to bear with me through some of that. Okay?

Good.

Now, we can really get started.

Our
Agreement
+++

Tom Watson & YOU

Chapter 2

BARK! SHAKE. RUMBLE.

On this day, Stick Dog and his buddies were all at his home playing a game. Stick Dog lives in a big pipe out in the woods and sleeps on an old couch cushion. The pipe is nice and dry, and the couch cushion is nice and cushy.

The game the five dogs were playing is called BARK! And the game goes like this: Whenever something moves anywhere—a leaf in the wind, a bird flying by, a triceratops charging out of the forest—

the first one to bark gets five points. The
second one to bark gets four points, the
third barker gets three points, and so on.
Whoever has the most points at the end
of the game is the winner.

Whenever you see two or more dogs
barking somewhere, odds are pretty good
that they are playing this game.

You should try it too. Get a friend or

a sister or a brother or a grandpa and play. Hold real still and then as soon as something moves, bark real loud a couple of times. Keep score and everything. A couple things to remember when you play this game: First, don't play it at school unless you want detention. Second, when you play this game, people are going to think you're crazy.

After a couple of hours of playing BARK!, the five buddies went down to the creek to get a nice cool drink of water. They walked into a shallow part of the creek, lowered their heads, and slurped away.

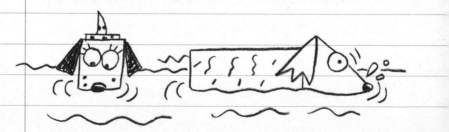

"Have you ever seen little humans drink?" Karen asked the others after getting her fill. Now, Karen is a dachshund, so it didn't take much to fill her up—several hearty mouthfuls and her thirst was quenched. "It's kind of strange."

"How so?" Stripes asked.

"They use this magic thing."

Mutt had now walked into a deeper part of the creek, cooling off his whole body in the slow-running water. "What do you mean?"

"Well, the obvious way to drink is like we're doing right now, of course," Karen began to explain. To demonstrate, she

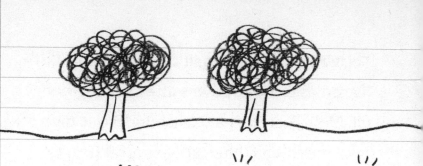

dropped her head and took a quick lap of water in her mouth and swallowed. "You know, find some liquid, lower your head, and drink. No big deal. But the way they do it is bizarre."

Mutt had risen, soaking wet, from the water and began to walk to the shore. "How's that?"

"It's crazy," Karen said. "I see little humans

do it at Picasso Park all the time. They have boxes that they shove magical sticks into."

"Magical?" Poo-Poo asked.

"Oh, yeah! Way magical," said Karen. "You should see them. They press their magic sticks into the boxes of liquid, then put their lips around one end of the stick and then the drink comes up! That's why it's magic. The liquid goes up!"

"It doesn't. No way," said Stripes.

"It does, I swear!" exclaimed Karen.

"That's impossible. Liquid can't go up. It only goes down," Mutt said. He had reached the shore now and climbed out of the creek. "Rain comes down. The creek runs from higher points to lower points. Liquids do not go up."

"I know that," said Karen. "That's what makes the sticks magical."

Now, this conversation would likely have continued for some time, but by now everybody had had a drink and gathered around Mutt. Stick Dog, Karen, Poo-Poo, and Stripes knew that he was soaking wet, and it was a very warm day.

"Ready?" Mutt asked.

They all nodded.

And Mutt gave a lengthy and mighty shake, showering the others with water droplets and cool, wet mist.

"That feels wonderful," Poo-Poo said.

"And smells even better," added Stripes.

As a token of gratitude for the cooling shower, everyone helped Mutt collect all the things that had sprayed out of his fur with the water. There was a pen cap, a shoelace, a broken Ping-Pong ball, and a Snickers candy bar wrapper.

Now cooled off, the dogs relaxed. With the rippling of the creek water splashing across the rocks and against the muddy banks, it was a lovely and peaceful place to be.

Until the peace and calmness were interrupted by two sounds.

The first sound was Stick Dog's stomach.

Stick Dog was hungry. And Stick Dog needed some food. And when Stick Dog

GRUMBLING NOISES

gets hungry, his four friends get hungry too.
That's just the way it happens.

It's kind of like when you're in class and
your teacher is up in the front going on
and on about how red and blue make
purple or three times three is nine or
how neat handwriting is, like, the most
important thing in the world. In fact,
without neat handwriting, the whole future

of the planet could be in jeopardy. If none
of us knows how to put that little extra
bumpy thing on a cursive Z, then the
whole world is going to collapse under
the horrible weight of bad penmanship.
If handwriting isn't neat, well, that's just
the end of everything. We all might as
well crawl into a hole and wait for the
inevitable crashing of all human life!

My teacher and I don't really see eye to eye on this subject.

Anyway, when one of those teachers is giving one of those lessons and everybody in class is getting a little sleepy and droopy eyed, something happens.

Do you know what it is?

Somebody yawns.

And when that somebody yawns, it sets off a gigantic chain reaction among all the students, and everybody starts yawning. And then the teacher turns around so nobody can see—and then the teacher yawns too.

Well, that's sort of what happened regarding Stick Dog's stomach. When it started to rumble, then all the stomachs of all the other dogs started to rumble too.

But that was just the first sound that interrupted their cooling break down by the creek. The other sound came from something none of the dogs had ever seen before.

And someone else had heard it too.

Chapter 3

WHAT IS A FRANKFURTER?

They heard a single, small bell.

Karen asked, "What's that jingling sound?"

Poo-Poo answered immediately, "Woo-hoo! It's Santa. It's his sleigh. Reindeer! Jingling bells! Doggie treats for everybody! Woo-hoo!"

"Umm, Poo-Poo?" said Stick Dog.

"Yes?"

"It's June twentieth."

"So?" said Poo-Poo. He was very

distracted and was barely listening to Stick

Dog at all. He was looking up at the sky,

swinging his head back and forth, looking

for Santa and his reindeer. "So what?"

"Umm, Christmas is in December," said Stick Dog. "You know, December twenty-fifth, when it's all cold and snowy and the humans have pine trees and lights up all over the place?"

Poo-Poo looked down at the ground. It sort of looked like he expected there to be snow all the way up to his knees. "It's not winter, is it?" Poo-Poo whispered, and looked glum. Then his voice grew louder, and he smiled a little bit. "Maybe Santa made a mistake."

"Does Santa ever make mistakes?" Stick Dog asked in the kind of way like everybody already knew the answer because it was so obvious.

"No," said Poo-Poo. Then he whispered, "He never does."

While Poo-Poo was hanging his head, the other dogs took turns guessing what it could be.

Karen said, "I think I know what that sound is."

"What is it?" Stick Dog asked.

"It's a giant flying cuckoo clock. Some of those things jingle. Maybe the little bird that pops out of the door and rings the bell when the hour changes has taken over the clock. And maybe it's flying somewhere above us, jingling its little bell whenever it wants—even if the long hand isn't straight up, meaning it's whatever o'clock! Maybe it's a cuckoo clock revolution!"

Stick Dog looked at Karen. Then he looked at her some more. "I must tell you, Karen," Stick Dog began. "I'm very impressed that you know how to tell time."

"Oh, sure. It comes naturally to me,"
Karen said, puffing out her little dachshund
chest. "I know all the o'clocks. Two o'clock.
Seven o'clock. Fifty-three o'clock. Tomato
o'clock. All of them!"

"I see," Stick Dog said very slowly. He then
waited a few seconds and added, "I really

like your idea about the cuckoo clock revolution and everything. It might be absolutely right. In fact, it probably is. But I was just wondering—Are those birds inside cuckoo clocks actually alive? Or are they just little, carved, wooden models?"

Karen whispered, "Little wooden models. I guess it's not a cuckoo bird revolution after all."

"But it was a good guess," encouraged Stick Dog.

"Yes. Yes, it was!" said Karen, feeling better already.

Now, Stripes and Mutt had their own ideas about that little jingling sound.

Stripes's theory was that a huge new species of miniature humans had emerged from beneath the earth and announced that they were going to take over the planet, ringing bells constantly to drive everybody crazy. Mutt's theory was different. He thought there might be a human riding a bike and ringing the bell on the handlebar.

"Those are two very different theories," said Stick Dog. "Why don't we go look?"

"Should we bring weapons?" asked Stripes.

"Why?" asked Stick Dog, cocking his head.

"Because," Stripes said, and then sighed as if this was the most ridiculous question

she had ever heard in her entire life.
"What if the new miniature, bell-ringing
humans are just over the hilltop? What if
they're ready to charge at us with all their
bell-ringing strength and ferocity? Don't
you think we should have weapons just in
case?"

Stick Dog considered this question for a moment, then said, "Yes, Stripes. I think that's a great idea. We should be prepared to meet and fight this new race of miniature, bell-ringing humans. Without question."

"Exactly!" Stripes exclaimed.

"Unfortunately," said Stick Dog, "we don't have any weapons. Never have."

"Darn it," said Stripes.

"But if we did, we would most certainly put them to use," said Stick Dog. "Come on, let's go check it out."

The five dogs ran from the creek and up

the hill to investigate the jingling sound.
They peeked over the top of the hill
and down the other side. There, they
discovered the source of that jingling bell.

It wasn't Santa Claus.

It wasn't a bicycle.

It wasn't a cuckoo clock revolution.

And it wasn't, believe it or not, a bunch of miniature humans emerging from underground to ring their bells and drive everybody crazy.

It was Peter.

Now, Stick Dog didn't know for sure that the man's name was Peter. But the side of his cart said "Peter's Frankfurters." So he just assumed that the man pushing the cart was named Peter. The cart was white, with printing on the side. There was an umbrella over the top of it. And it had four big wheels. Peter was pushing it and ringing an attached bell.

"That's the strangest contraption I've ever seen," said Poo-Poo. "Is it a car, a bike, a wheelbarrow? What?"

The five dogs peered over the hill and watched this strange man with the strange cart.

"What's a 'frankfurter'?" asked Karen.

"I have no idea," said Stick Dog.

Now, I know what you're going to say.
You're going to say, "Oh, yeah, right. The
dogs are reading now. They went to school
and learned phonics, and they know the
alphabet and they can read everything—
billboards, hot-dog carts, encyclopedias.
Like I'm going to believe that."

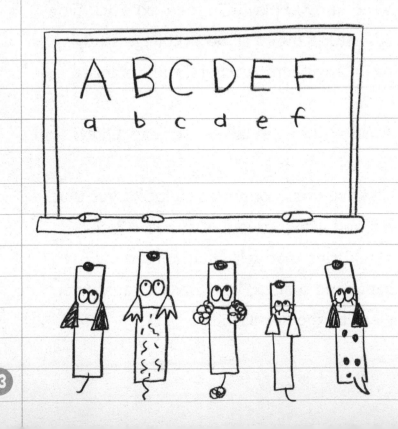

Well, come on now. These dogs have been talking in this story for a while now. Actually, I've been interpreting for them, if you want to get picky. So, if they can talk, they might as well be able to read. And I don't mean to be rude here, but you did agree not to bug me about every tiny detail. Remember?

Who knows? Maybe in the next Stick Dog adventure, they'll all be in college studying to be engineers, teachers, and botanists.

Anyway, they can talk—and read. Okay?

The five dogs continued to look over that hill, and every couple of minutes Peter would ring that bell. Then, something happened that explained what frankfurters were to the five friends.

A boy came up to Peter and asked him
something. They talked for a minute, and
the boy gave him a dollar. And Peter gave
him something back. The boy sniffed at it
and then took a great big bite. And smiled.

"What is that?" asked Karen.

"That must be a frankfurter," said Stick
Dog.

"Can you smell that?" asked Stripes, suddenly licking her lips. "It smells superb-i-melicious."

Stick Dog looked at Stripes but didn't say anything. He knew "superb-i-melicious" was not a word. But he also knew that if it was a word, then it would be the most accurate word to describe the wonderful aromas emanating from that frankfurter cart. His stomach began to growl even louder than before.

Stick Dog firmly stated, "We have to get some of those."

Now, before we continue, you all know what a frankfurter is, right? It's a fancy name for a hot dog. I'm calling them "frankfurters" in this story because using "hot dog" could get a little confusing—or at least a little too repetitive. There would be too many "dogs" everywhere. So we're using the word "frankfurter."

And Stick Dog's right: They really are delicious. With a little ketchup and mustard, mm-mmm. On a nice, soft, doughy bun. Maybe a little cut-up dill pickle. Oh,

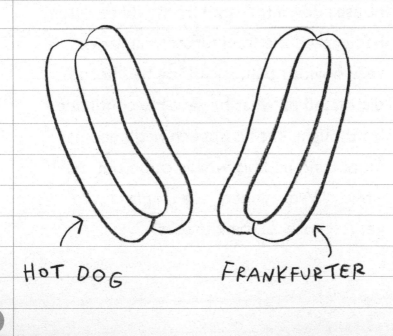

HOT DOG   FRANKFURTER

yeah, that's what I'm talking about. A sprinkle of salt. Maybe just a little shredded cheddar cheese on the top. Superb-i-melicious indeed.

"We need a plan," said Stick Dog. It was just then, however, that something caught his eye as he spied the frankfurter cart as a potential food target. It was a slight movement among the branches of a maple tree. The tree itself was a few houses down the road from where Peter had parked the frankfurter cart. It was very obvious that Stick Dog had become distracted by what he saw. He continued his thought, but his speech had become monotone, and his words came out much slower. "We . . . need . . . a . . . plan . . . to . . . get . . . those . . . frankfurters."

"What is it, Stick Dog?" Mutt asked as he stepped closer. He had noticed Stick Dog's change in demeanor.

Poo-Poo, Karen, and Stripes noticed as well. There was a sudden nervousness among them. It was quite unusual, they knew, to see Stick Dog lose his focus—especially when food was involved.

"I saw something in that tree," he whispered. "It's about four houses down the road from Peter, the frankfurter man. In the maple tree there by the road."

The other four dogs instantly turned their heads in that direction.

"How far up?" Mutt asked.

"About five or six branches from the bottom," Stick Dog answered. He had not stopped staring at the spot. "On the left side."

As everyone calculated this and peered in that specific area, a branch there shook a little and then the branch below it shook a lot—as if something had moved from one tree limb to another.

"If it's a squirrel," said Poo-Poo, "I'll take care of this problem in a jiffy. That maniacal little nutkin doesn't stand a chance with old Mr. Poo-Poo on the case!"

This startled Stick Dog out of his trance. His voice and speech pattern normalized. "It's not a squirrel," he said quickly. Stick Dog didn't want Poo-Poo charging out of the woods and barking up at the tree. That would definitely put Peter on alert—and ruin any chance they had of getting those frankfurters. "I saw a strange set of eyes. Not a squirrel's eyes or a bird's. Something different."

They all continued to stare at those upper branches.

But only for three seconds.

That's because, after three seconds, a pair of black eyes poked their way through some maple leaves. There was no doubt what those eyes were staring at—they were staring at the frankfurter cart. And seconds later, a narrow gray nose emerged beneath the eyes and began sniffing and twitching.

"Somebody else is after the frankfurters," whispered Stick Dog. When he said this, the face of their competition revealed itself fully.

"It's a bandit!" yelled Stripes.

"Shh!" said Stick Dog.

In rapid succession, the others guessed at the identity of the thing in the tree.

"It's a burglar!" said Poo-Poo. "It's wearing a mask!"

"It's a masked madman!" Mutt guessed.

Then Karen said, "It's an inchworm!"

At this, they all turned to their dachshund comrade.

"It's not an inchworm, Karen," sighed Poo-Poo. "It's way too big. It's black and white and gray, not green. And it's wearing a mask—an evil mask of some sort."

"No, not in the tree!" Karen giggled. "Here on the ground on this rock. I love these little guys. The way they move cracks me up. Look! Up and down, up and down, up and down. Just to go the tiniest distance. I mean, grow some legs, little fellah! You know what I mean?!"

Stick Dog stared at Karen only for a moment. She was certainly going to be occupied with that inchworm for a while. He turned to the others.

"It's not a masked madman or a burglar or a bandit," he said.

"What is it?" Mutt, Stripes, and Poo-Poo asked in unison.

Off to the side, Karen dropped her head lower toward the rock. The others could hear her. "Up and down, up and down." She giggled. "You're really moving now, little inchie!"

"It's a raccoon," Stick Dog answered. "And it has its eyes on those frankfurters just like we do."

Poo-Poo was surprised. "I thought raccoons only came out at night."

"That's the only time I've ever seen them," confirmed Stick Dog. "This one's different, I guess. It must be really hungry."

"Why, that little scavenger!" Poo-Poo exclaimed. He was now more aghast than surprised. "Imagine, just imagine, what it's up to. Looking for food wherever he can find it! Stealing it! Eating it! What kind of a nasty little beast would act like that?!"

Stick Dog didn't answer, but he did smile a bit to himself.

"I have a right mind to warn the

frankfurter man about this ring-tailed menace," Poo-Poo continued. There was little doubt that Poo-Poo was greatly offended by the raccoon's interest in the frankfurters.

"It's all right, it's all right," Stick Dog said in a calming voice. "We have a little competition, that's all. It's nothing we can't handle."

By this time, the inchworm had made its way off the rock and Karen had rejoined the group.

"We need a plan to get those frankfurters," Stick Dog said again.

Thankfully, his four friends had four fantastic plans.

Chapter 4

STICK DOG CANNOT FLY A HELICOPTER

"I've got it," said Mutt. He looked excited. "They're called 'frankfurters,' right?"

"Right," said Stick Dog.

"Okay, here's the plan," Mutt continued. "We walk up to the guy. What's his name? Is it Pumpkin-Head?"

"Peter," said Stick Dog.

"Yeah, yeah. That's what I meant." Mutt nodded. "And we say we're all from the same family. And we say our last name is Furter. Like, you're Stick Dog Furter. And I'm Mutt Furter. And we introduce Poo-Poo Furter, Stripes Furter, and Karen Furter."

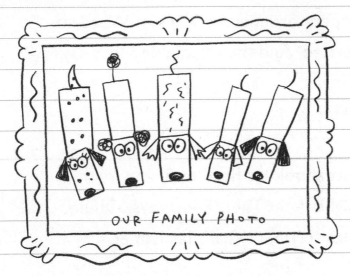

OUR FAMILY PHOTO

"Go on," Stick Dog said real slowly. It appeared he didn't like where this whole idea was going.

"Then," said Mutt, "we tell Pumpkin-Head ..."

"Peter."

"Yeah, Peter. We say, 'Hey, Peter. We're missing a member of our family. We desperately need to find him. We're so worried.' And then Pumpkin-Head says ..."

"Peter."

Mutt shook his head back and forth. "Right, Peter. Then, Peter says, 'Oh no, that's terrible. What's his name?'"

Stick Dog, Karen, Stripes, and Poo-Poo all stared at Mutt. But he didn't say anything.

"And?" asked Stick Dog finally.

"And," said Mutt, getting excited. "We say, 'Frank!' Frank Furter! Get it? Frankfurter! Then we say, 'Have you seen any Frank Furters around here, Pumpkin-Head?' And he says, 'Boy, have I! I've seen about fifty frankfurters right here in this cart. And since they're all members of your family, you should take them home with you.'"

Stick Dog closed his eyes. "Umm."

"Yeah?" said Mutt. He was very excited. "It's great, isn't it?"

"It is great," said Stick Dog, trying to let him down easy. "It's great in a sort of non-great way. Sort of. Umm, yeah."

"What do you mean?" asked Mutt, tilting his head a little to the left.

"Well, we don't really look like we're all from the same family," Stick Dog said, nodding his head toward each of them. "It's hard for a Dalmatian, dachshund, poodle, mutt, and whatever-I-am to be from the same family."

"Umm, HEL-LO!" Mutt said. "Adoption? Ever hear of it?"

Stick Dog nodded his head. "I have heard of it, yes. And that may explain all of us being from the same family, but that still doesn't explain how a rolled-up piece of meat stuck in a folded-up piece of bread is related to us."

This seemed to suddenly make sense to Mutt. "Not going to work?"

"Oh, I'm not saying that at all," said Stick Dog. "But because there is just a sliver of doubt about its feasibility, maybe we should listen to some other ideas too."

Mutt nodded his head. "Sounds reasonable."

"Never fear," declared Poo-Poo. "I know exactly how to get those frankfurters."

"Let's hear it," said Stick Dog. And Karen, Stripes, and a somewhat-dejected Mutt all nodded along in agreement.

"Well, you remember how we got those hamburgers at Picasso Park that one day?" Poo-Poo began. They all remembered because it was, of course, one of the best days of their entire lives.

"Yes, we remember," answered Stick Dog.

"How could we forget?" said Karen, a little drool falling down to the ground from the corner of her mouth. Now, that's really not all that disgusting, because Karen is, after all, a dachshund—so the drool didn't have all that far to fall. Now, if the drool was falling, say, from the corner of *your* mouth? That would be gross.

"Well," Poo-Poo continued. "We get a bunch more of those hamburgers, and we slowly saunter by Piddly-Pants there."

"You mean Peter."

"Yeah, Peter. We saunter by Peter, eating those hamburgers real casual-like. Really enjoying them, you know? Groaning and moaning about how super-tasty they are. Letting some of that meaty hamburger juice drip down our chins. Yeah, that's what we do."

"Umm," started Stick Dog. Then he waited a minute and asked, "Why?"

"Why?"

"Yeah. Why?"

"Don't you see?" asked Poo-Poo, sounding exasperated. "Piddly-Pants sells frankfurters. Hamburgers are probably the natural enemy to someone who sells frankfurters. If he sees that we're all enjoying a bunch of delicious hamburgers, he'll want to convince us that we're wrong. He'll want to convince us that frankfurters are so much better. And to do that, he'll dish out frankfurters to us by the dozen! We'll be eating frankfurters for hours."

"Poo-Poo?"

"You don't have to say it, Stick Dog," said Poo-Poo proudly. "I know it's a great plan. You don't have to congratulate me or anything."

"We don't have any hamburgers," said Stick Dog. "And if we did have hamburgers, we wouldn't really be worried about getting frankfurters. You know what I mean? And his name is Peter, not Piddly-Pants."

Poo-Poo looked a little sad—and a little disappointed—when Stick Dog pointed out this flaw in his plan. Stick Dog saw this and added, "You know, Poo-Poo, that's a really sophisticated plan you came up with. Using the hamburgers as a way to stir the jealousy instincts in a human has probably never been considered before. You are, no doubt, the only creature on the planet who could come up with it."

Poo-Poo lifted his head. A smile had returned to his face. "I am quite unique, aren't I?"

"Without question," answered Stick Dog, and then he turned to the others. "Well, does anybody have any other ideas?"

"I do," said Stripes. "I do indeed."

Stick Dog inhaled a great big breath and asked, "What is it?"

Stripes smirked a little bit, smiling from one corner of her mouth. She was obviously very pleased with herself. "The first thing we need," said Stripes, "is a helicopter. Then ..."

"Stop right there," said Stick Dog.

"Yes?"

"Where are we going to get a helicopter?"

When Stripes looked at Stick Dog, you could tell she thought Stick Dog wasn't very bright at all. "The helicopter store. Where else?"

"There's no such place as a helicopter store," sighed Stick Dog.

But by this time, Stripes was already chattering ahead with her plan. "We take the helicopter. And we fly it over to Patsy Puffenstuff over there."

"His name's Peter."

"Whatever," said Stripes. "We hover the

helicopter over the frankfurter cart.
Then a couple of us get lowered down
on a rope ladder from the open door of
the helicopter. While Patsy Puffenstuff is
getting totally blown
away by the wind from
the helicopter blades,
we snatch all the
frankfurters we can
grab. One of us pulls the
others back up; we land
the helicopter by Stick
Dog's house and have
the feast of a lifetime."

Mutt, Karen, and Poo-
Poo were all nodding
along in agreement with
Stripes. And the more Stripes got excited,

the more the three of them got excited
too. By the time Stripes had provided the
final details of her plan, she was jumping up
and down in place.

She yelled, "Off to the helicopter store!
Follow me!"

Poo-Poo, Mutt, and Karen wheeled around
to take off after her.

"Stop," said Stick Dog calmly. "Where are
you going?"

"The helicopter store," answered Mutt,
skidding to a stop just after he had taken
a few quick steps. The other dogs stopped
too.

"There's no such thing," said Stick Dog.

"Sure there is," said Mutt, but he was starting to sound a little doubtful. He knew that Stick Dog was usually right about such things.

"Where is it?"

"Well," said Mutt, and then he paused for a moment. "I'm not positive. But Stripes knows. Yeah, that's it! Stripes knows! We're all following Stripes."

"What the heck, let's say there is such a thing as a helicopter store," said Stick Dog. "Can you tell me where it is, Stripes? Where is it that you are running off to just now?"

"I'm . . . not . . . sure," answered Stripes, then she gained her confidence back a little. "To the mall. I bet there's a helicopter store at the mall. That's where we're going. You betcha."

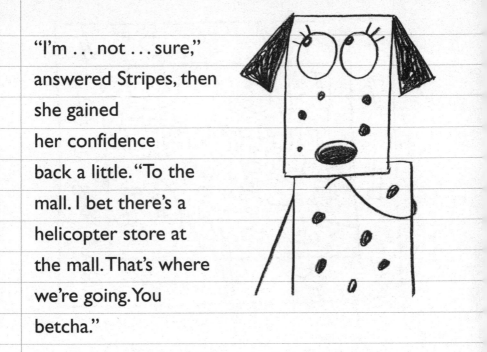

"Umm, okay," said Stick Dog. "Let's go ahead and say that there's such a thing as a helicopter store. And let's assume that just such a store is at our local shopping mall. After all, that mall has about every other kind of store. So why not a helicopter store? How much does a helicopter cost anyway?"

"A dollar?" answered Stripes. "Two dollars? Maybe? We can probably find that much change in the parking lot."

"I think it may cost a little more than that. But you know what? I've never bought a helicopter before, so what do I know?"

"Maybe they're having a big sale today,"

said Mutt, trying to help.

"Maybe so," said Stick Dog. "So let's go ahead and say there is such a thing as a helicopter store. And let's say there is one at the mall. And let's say it costs one dollar—because of the big helicopter sale today. I still have one question."

Stripes closed her eyes. She really, really, really didn't want to know what Stick Dog's next question was. "Yes?"

"Do any of us know how to fly a helicopter?"

Stripes kicked at some dirt with her front left paw. "Shoot," she said, and hung her head.

"If it wasn't for that one detail," said Stick Dog.

Then Stripes lifted her head and started to smile a little to herself just for a moment before straightening her face again. "I thought YOU knew how to fly a helicopter, Stick Dog."

Stick Dog began to shake his head and speak, but he didn't get the chance because Stripes turned to the other three dogs and began speaking herself.

"Forget it, you guys," she said, and sort of nodded a couple of times toward Stick Dog. "The helicopter plan isn't going to work, after all. I had everything all worked out, but Stick Dog doesn't know how to be a helicopter pilot. So the plan is ruined. Thanks to him."

"But . . . ," began Stick Dog.

But Stripes interrupted him again. "No, no," she said. "Don't worry about it, Stick Dog. You don't have to apologize to me. It's okay. I'm not mad at you for ruining my most excellent plan with your lack of helicopter-piloting skills. Oh, I am a little disappointed in you, that's true. But not mad. You're still my good friend. I do wish I could depend on you to do your part when it comes to such things, but it's okay. We'll get through it."

Stick Dog just stared. And stared. Finally, he said, "Well, Stripes, I don't know what to say."

"You don't have to say anything," said Stripes. "It's okay."

"Thanks," said Stick Dog. And then he turned to Karen. "You must have a plan too. Is it a good plan?"

"It's not a good plan. It's not even a great

plan," said Karen. "It is definitely the most extra-spectacular splendiferous frankfurter-snatching strategy of all time."

"Okay," Stick Dog said. "Out with it then."

"It's so brilliant because it's so simple," Karen began, and started to pace in front of the other four dogs. "We're going to walk right up to old Prickle Pop there and ..."

"His name's Peter," Stick Dog whispered.

"Mm-hmm, yeah. That's what I said," replied Karen, never missing one of her little dachshund strides. "Anyway, this marvelous plan is going to work for one reason: greed."

"Greed?" asked Stick Dog.

"Greed," answered Karen. Then she did something rather odd. And, let's face it, rather odd for this bunch of dogs is going to be pretty darn peculiar. Karen stopped pacing back and forth and said, "Watch this."

Stick Dog, Poo-Poo, Mutt, and Stripes all watched as Karen proceeded to drop down on the ground and tuck her little dachshund legs up close to her long dachshund tummy. Then she curled her tail up underneath and between her legs. Finally, she tucked her chin close to her chest and, trying not to move her lips at all, said, "What am I?"

"A dachshund who just forgot how to walk," guessed Mutt.

"No."

"Ooh! I love guessing games," said Poo-Poo. "You're a furry torpedo!"

"No."

Stripes walked a couple of circles around Karen, staring down and examining her the whole time. "I think I got it," she said. "You're a gorilla who fell asleep wearing a dachshund costume."

"No!" said Karen, feeling a little exasperated. "Stick Dog? Do you have a guess?"

Stick Dog did indeed have a guess. He wanted to say, "You are the weirdest dog on the planet!"—but he didn't. He simply said, "No, I don't have a guess. I give up. What are you?"

"Duh," said Karen, lifting her little chin up slightly and looking at herself. "I'm a frankfurter! See the color!? The shape!? Everything?!"

"Umm, okay," said Stick Dog. "You're an awfully large frankfurter, by the way. But let's try and see past that. Let's say everybody—including Peter—believes you are a frankfurter. What's the rest of your plan after you're done imitating a frankfurter?"

Karen looked at Stick Dog like his brain had just turned into a rawhide chew. She sighed. "Do I really have to explain it? It's so simple."

"Umm, yes," said Stick Dog. "Please explain it."

"When Prickle Pop . . ."

"Peter," corrected Stick Dog.

"Right, right. That's what I said," said Karen. "When he sees me, he's going to think he hit the jackpot. I'll be the world-record, biggest frankfurter he's ever seen. He'll do anything to have me. Think about it: His whole world revolves around frankfurters. And when he sees me, his greed will overtake him. He'll do anything to get me. You can trade me in for all the other frankfurters!"

They just looked at Karen, so she continued with her plan.

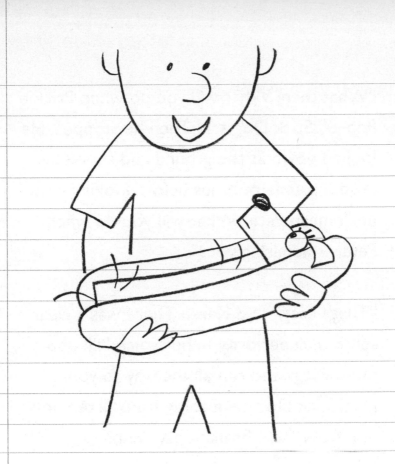

"After you get those frankfurters from the cart, he'll put me down to admire me. He'll think he is in some crazy, beautiful dream with the world's largest, most magnificent frankfurter right there for him to have and to hold."

"What then? What will you do when Prickle Pop—" Stick Dog said. Then he stopped. He looked down at the ground and shook his head a couple of times before looking back up. "I mean Peter. What will you do when Peter is admiring you?"

"That's easy," said Karen. There was a clear sense of superiority in her voice. "I'll pop out my legs and run all the way to your pipe, Stick Dog. Save some frankfurters for me! Yeah, baby! Brilliant plan, huh?"

Stick Dog had grown more and more impatient. And his stomach had grown more and more grumbly. He usually tried to be polite when one of his friends had a plan that was a little, umm, not so good. But now he had just had enough.

When was the last time you had had enough? I'll tell you mine. I was taking out the garbage. Do you have to take out the garbage? Well, I do.

It was one of those big, white, plastic, stretchy bags from the kitchen garbage can. It had a bunch of old food and paper and old cleaning rags in it. And my mom had just dumped all the dust and yuck from the vacuum cleaner in there. You know that big, gray clump of grossness that has dust and hair and shoe mud all swirled around inside it like a tornado? The bag was full of it along with all the other garbage stuff.

So I'm taking it out to the end of the driveway, right? Only it's really heavy this time. Now, I'm pretty strong. I can break a stick in half right over my knee! How about that? Yeah, it's true—totally true.

Anyway, I'm strong.

But that garbage bag was real heavy, so I had to sort of drag it to the can instead of carry it. And about halfway down the driveway, it started tearing. Only I didn't know it started tearing. So by the time I got to the can, most of the garbage was spread out behind me in a line on the driveway.

And—NO!—I didn't happen to notice that the bag was getting lighter. So please don't ask.

Well, I had to go pick up all that filth and yuck with my hands. Back and forth, back and forth, back and forth until it was all back in the bag. I was so mad that I kicked the bag.

And all the dust and hair from the vacuum cleaner came POOFing out in a great cloud of terrible-ness right into my face.

That was the last time I had had enough.

All of a sudden, I feel like taking a shower.

So this time, it was Stick Dog who had
had enough. He looked at Karen, who was
still kind of strutting around about the
genius-ness of her plan. Stick Dog just said,
"Frankfurters don't have fur. Peter will never
believe it."

All four of the other dogs looked at Stick
Dog with their heads sort of turned
sideways like he was speaking a foreign
language—like cat language or turtle
language or pumpkin language.

"What is it?" Stick Dog asked.

They all asked at the same time, "Who is
Peter?"

Stick Dog closed his eyes for a moment
and then opened them slowly, very slowly.
"Peter is the man over there with the
frankfurter cart. Remember?"

Then all four of them started nodding
their heads with great energy and
enthusiasm.

"Okay. Those were four great plans—really,
they were," Stick Dog said with as much
sincerity as he could muster. "But I think I

have a plan that might just work, if you all agree."

"What's your plan?" asked Poo-Poo. Stripes, Mutt, and Karen had gathered around Stick Dog to listen.

"Well, look over there. See where Peter has his frankfurter cart parked?" Stick Dog said. And before he could be interrupted, he added, "Peter is the one working at the cart."

The four other dogs looked over at the cart and then back at Stick Dog.

"Well, somebody is drying their clothes in the yard right next to where he's parked. See the clothes and sheets and stuff flapping in the wind? And there's a basket of folded laundry too. I think we can sneak around the back of that blue house to right where all those clothes are hanging. We'll get behind one of those two sheets hanging there. As soon as he turns his head to look in the other direction, we'll pounce out from behind the laundry, grab some frankfurters, and run like crazy."

Stick Dog looked to see the reactions of his four friends.

"What a lousy plan," said Karen.

"All of our plans were much more sophisticated and brilliant," said Mutt.

"What a bogus plan," said Poo-Poo.

"Pretty simple, isn't it?" sighed Stripes.

Stick Dog gathered himself together a
little bit. He wanted those frankfurters
really badly. And he wanted to end this
conversation almost as much. So all he
said was "You're right. You're right. You're
all correct. It's not a very good plan at
all. It's rather simple and boring. And
your plans were all so much better in
so many ways. But I wonder if we could
just try mine out? Could we? Are you
with me?"

It was just the kind of encouragement they needed.

"Yes!" they all shouted together.

After they calmed down a little, Mutt asked, "Stick Dog?"

"Yes?"

Mutt glanced down the street, then quickly back at Stick Dog. "I think we better hurry."

"Why?"

"That raccoon is getting closer to the frankfurter cart."

Stick Dog could instantly see that Mutt was

correct. He had been
so busy listening to his
friends' plans that Stick
Dog had neglected to
keep a watchful eye
on the raccoon. It was
no longer in the maple

tree four houses away from the cart. It
was now in a pine tree three houses away.

The others saw it, as well.

Poo-Poo couldn't stand it. "Errgh!" he
snarled, and began pacing. "It's getting
closer. It's going to get there first! What
are we going to do, Stick Dog?"

"It's okay," Stick Dog said. "But we do need
to hurry."

"We need to do something else too," added Karen.

"What's that?" Stripes asked, and tilted her head.

"We need to give the raccoon a name," she said simply.

"A name?"

"Oh, yeah," said Karen as if this was a perfectly logical thing to do. "If we're going to have a nemesis who is trying to snatch what is rightfully ours, it needs to have a name—an evil name."

Stick Dog could hardly believe what he was hearing. They had to hurry. He knew that

raccoons were quite capable of finding and retrieving food. He'd seen enough toppled trash cans and ripped-open garbage bags to know that. He also knew that raccoons had powerful, sharp claws. He'd seen plenty of tracks in the woods and outside his pipe below Highway 16. He did not want to mess with a raccoon—and he certainly didn't want one to get the frankfurters before they did.

But instead of hustling along with their plan, they were going to waste precious time naming the raccoon. He was just about to put a stop to this nonsense when Mutt spoke up.

"I have a problem with this whole naming business," said Mutt.

Stick Dog exhaled a little to himself. Finally, someone else saw how silly this was.

"What is it, Mutt?"

"Well, we don't know if our new raccoon enemy is a boy or a girl," he explained. "That's going to make it difficult to come up with a name."

Karen, Poo-Poo, and Stripes nodded in complete understanding. Stick Dog just stood there getting hungrier. He was trying not to let his frustration show.

Karen, who had come up with the whole naming idea, took charge of the conversation. "Look, let's just throw out some name suggestions for the evil raccoon and see what works best," she said. "Remember the whole boy-girl problem as you make your suggestions. Try to stay away from names that are too girl- or boy-specific."

This seemed to make good sense to the others. Even Stick Dog agreed, but solely because he wanted to move the give-the-raccoon-food-snatcher-a-name process along as fast as possible.

The suggestions came at a furious pace from all of them except Stick Dog.

"DespicaBeast!"

"Masked Mobster!"

"Racc-a-Doom!"

"Devil-Meister!"

"The Raccoon Typhoon!"

While Stick Dog listened to these and other suggestions, his stomach became impatient. It grumbled loudly. It was as if his body was telling him to put an end to all this naming business.

"Okay, guys," he interjected in a firm but friendly voice. "Those are all great suggestions. But we better get moving here. The next name is the winner."

You would think that would make them all blurt out a choice quickly. But the opposite was actually true. There was a slight hesitation as they each considered and tried to come up with something really good. But it was Mutt who spoke up first. And it was Mutt who chose the name of their new raccoon nemesis.

It was Mutt who said, "Phyllis!"

"Phyllis it is," Stick Dog said instantly, before anyone could object. He nodded toward the house with the drying laundry in the yard. "This way, as fast as we can!"

As if to add a greater sense of urgency and a spirit of teamwork, Karen exclaimed, "Down with Phyllis!"

And they took off.

Chapter 5

KAREN IS GONE

They tore as fast as they could around to the back of the blue house. When they got there, they slowed down and stalked their way to the corner so that they could just see where Peter had his frankfurter cart parked on the sidewalk.

"Okay," said Stick Dog. "First, we need to get closer. When he turns his head, we run behind the hanging laundry. Let's get behind one of those big white sheets. Got it?"

"Got it," the other four said.

"We better go one at a time. There will be less chance of us getting spotted that way," Stick Dog said. "Karen, since you're the smallest, you should go first."

Karen raced across the green lawn, pumping her little dachshund legs as fast as she could. In a matter of seconds, she was positioned behind one of the sheets hanging out to dry. She turned around to face the others, waved to indicate the

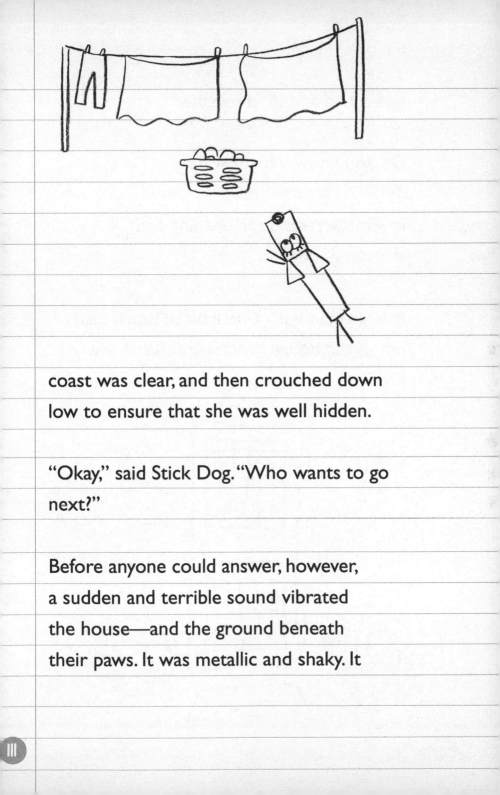

coast was clear, and then crouched down
low to ensure that she was well hidden.

"Okay," said Stick Dog. "Who wants to go
next?"

Before anyone could answer, however,
a sudden and terrible sound vibrated
the house—and the ground beneath
their paws. It was metallic and shaky. It

screeched and then smashed.

Do you know what it was?

It was a screen door opening and
slamming shut.

A large man with a dark black beard came
out of the house, stomping toward where

Karen was hiding behind the hanging sheet.

She had heard the bang and jerked her
head in the direction of the sound. But
behind the hanging sheet, she could not
see this large, impending doom. She turned
to look at Mutt, Stripes, Stick Dog, and
Poo-Poo.

While Karen could see nothing, the other
dogs could see everything. They saw the

large, bearded man coming toward the
laundry—coming closer toward Karen.
They began waving their paws in the air,
signaling Karen the best they could about
the approaching danger.

She knew she had to run—or hide. Her
legs were already tired, and they felt heavy
and frozen from fright. Karen could feel
the giant human creature coming closer

even though she couldn't see him. The rumbles and vibrations in the ground grew more severe with each additional footfall.

She snapped her head back toward her friends one final time before taking action. The other dogs were still waving frantically, but they knew they couldn't bark and give themselves away to the bearded beast.

Karen couldn't get her legs to run.

But she could hide.

And hide she did.

The stomping human was three steps away, shielded from seeing Karen only by the thin cotton sheet hanging from the clothesline.

Karen leaped higher than she ever had
before—at least ten inches—above the
laundry basket.

The human creature was two steps away.

Karen dove nose-first into the clean, dry
clothes.

He was one step away.

Karen dug and nestled herself into the

bottom of the basket, wriggling beneath all the folded napkins, blue jeans, T-shirts, and underwear.

The bearded man opened his fist and stretched his thick fingers wide, preparing to grab and clench. He grasped the sheet in his hand and rubbed it between his fingers. "Still damp," he said to himself, and looked up at the sky.

Karen knew she was safe. If the laundry was still damp on the line, this scary, bearded human beast would leave the basket. He'd come back later when everything was dry and then fill up the basket and take it in. She could relax. They could get back to their frankfurter plan. They could beat Phyllis the raccoon to the delicious-smelling food. Karen was closer to the frankfurter cart than before. She could smell that meaty aroma all the better now. She wiped a little drool from her mouth on a white linen napkin in the bottom of the basket.

Then the basket moved.

In a voice that was dark and gravelly, deep and foreboding, the human said, "Might as well take these in."

With that, the basket—and Karen—were up in the air.

The man held the basket on his hip, pivoted in place, and began his return to the house. Halfway across the lawn, Karen stuck her head out from the back of the basket. There was a pair of boxer shorts decorated with lots of red hearts on top of her head. She stared with wide eyes at the other dogs at the corner of the house. There was panic and fear on Karen's face—and there was panic and fear on the others' faces as they watched from a distance.

The screen door screeched again on its hinges as it opened.

Karen ducked her head beneath the underwear again. The man stepped inside. When the screen door slammed shut, the house and the ground shook.

Karen was gone.

Chapter 6

A DONKEY?

"What are we going to do?" Mutt asked. "She doesn't stand a chance against that guy!"

"Did you see the size of him?!" Stripes exclaimed.

"He's a giant!" Poo-Poo confirmed.

"Shh. Keep it down. Let me think," Stick Dog said quickly.

All of them were edgy and nervous. Every movement they made, from an ear scratch to a head turn, was sudden and fast.

"Does anyone have a chain saw?" asked Poo-Poo.

"Why?" asked Stripes.

"I was going to cut a hole in the side of the house to get Karen out."

"Good idea," said Stripes. "But I don't have one."

Mutt said, "I'm fresh out of chain saws."

"How about a motorcycle helmet?"

"Why?" asked Mutt.

"I was going to strap it on," said Poo-Poo. He demonstrated with his paws, placing an imaginary helmet on his head. "And then run repeatedly into the house until I made a hole. Then we could pull Karen out. I'm prepared to do it without the helmet, of course."

"You are great at smashing into things headfirst," said Stripes with genuine admiration. "But I don't have one."

Mutt spread out his legs and shook his entire body vigorously for seven seconds. From his tangled fur fell an old rubber ball, a pen cap, two bottle caps, a shoelace, and a yellow marker. He looked around at the stuff scattered on the ground. You could tell he was hoping to find a motorcycle helmet. There was great disappointment on his face when he realized there wasn't one. "Nothing," he said.

Stick Dog was still thinking.

Poo-Poo grew increasingly frustrated as his ideas failed to work out. "I'm just going to bark my head off," he said suddenly. "I don't know what else to do."

"Great idea," said Stripes.

"I'm in," Mutt said, clearing his throat.

All three dogs took deep inhales of air.

"Stop," said Stick Dog calmly. "Don't bark."

Stripes, Mutt, and Poo-Poo exhaled.

"Why not?" asked Stripes. "We're dogs. That's what we're supposed to do."

"Look," Stick Dog said. "We're going to rescue Karen; don't worry. But we have to be smart and quiet about it. Barking is only going to attract attention—from the giant bearded man; from Peter, the frankfurter man; and from all the neighbors around here. It might even alert Phyllis to our presence. And we don't want that."

"Good point," said Mutt.

"Now, let's check out the back of the house and try to see inside," said Stick Dog, crouching down to drag himself slowly and silently on his belly. The other dogs copied him. "Once we get a look inside, maybe we'll figure out a good way to get Karen back."

They slithered around the corner to the back of the house. There they found a small patio with a grill, two chairs, and a table.

"Look! A grill!" said Stripes. "Remember those hamburgers from the grill at Picasso Park? Oh, man, that was good eating. Best things I ever tasted."

"I can remember that glorious day," said Poo-Poo, closing his eyes and imagining.

Mutt was moving his jaw up and down slightly—almost like he was chewing. "Sometimes I dream about hamburgers."

"Hey, umm, guys?" Stick Dog said.

"I can almost taste them," Stripes whispered, now swaying slowly back and forth.

"Me too," moaned Mutt and Poo-Poo together.

"You guys! Snap out of it!" Stick Dog declared. "We have to rescue Karen."

They all opened their eyes at once and shook their heads. "Sorry, Stick Dog," Mutt said. "It's just that we saw the grill and everything. We couldn't help ourselves."

"It's okay. Follow me."

Luckily, there was a sliding glass door that led from the house to the patio. They scooched across the patio and peered inside.

"There she is," whispered Stick Dog.

"Where?" Mutt asked.

"Still in the laundry basket," answered Stick Dog. "See? The clothes are moving up and down every time she breathes."

"How do you know that's Karen?" asked Stripes.

"Yeah, Stick Dog," added Poo-Poo. "How do you know?"

Stick Dog turned his head and looked at them both. "We just saw her jump in the laundry basket a minute ago. Then we saw the basket get carried inside the house by the big guy with the beard. Now we see the basket inside, and there's something moving under the clothes. It's Karen."

"It could be somebody else," said Stripes. "We don't know for sure."

"Of course we know," said Stick Dog.

"But without seeing her," said Mutt, "we don't *know* know."

"Yes, we do," said Stick Dog.

"It really could be anyone," added Poo-Poo.

"It could be a chipmunk maybe. Or a donkey."

"A donkey?" Stick Dog asked, closing his eyes and trying to keep his composure.

"A small donkey, sure," Poo-Poo said matter-of-factly. "Stranger things have happened."

Stick Dog took a deep breath. "I'm not sure that's true."

"Karen could have *transformed* into a donkey," said Mutt, trying to help.

This made Stripes want to help too. "Or maybe she's been a donkey the whole time we've known her," she said. "But just wearing a dachshund costume."

"Yeah," said Poo-Poo, "what about that?"

Stick Dog couldn't even speak. He had to think—and act—fast. He had to end this conversation, help Karen, and then, finally, get to the frankfurters—before Phyllis. His stomach felt completely empty.

He tapped the glass door with his front right paw as lightly as he could while still making a noise. When he did, Karen

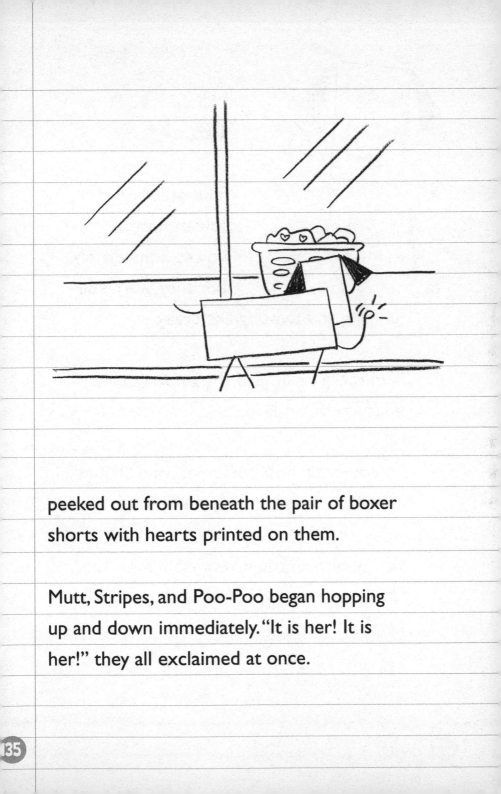

peeked out from beneath the pair of boxer
shorts with hearts printed on them.

Mutt, Stripes, and Poo-Poo began hopping
up and down immediately. "It is her! It is
her!" they all exclaimed at once.

"Shhh," said Stick Dog.

The other dogs lowered their voices immediately, but they were still jumping and twisting like crazy.

"I'm really, really glad she's not a donkey," whispered Poo-Poo.

"It could still be a costume," said Stripes. "But I'm pretty sure it's not."

"Okay, okay. Settle down," said Stick Dog. "Now that we found her, we have to save her."

Chapter 7

SOMEONE SEEKS A GIRLFRIEND

Karen stared at them from under the heart-decorated boxer shorts. She inched out a little farther. Her eyes darted quickly left and right, and then she hopped from the basket. She was excited to see her friends and began trotting happily toward them.

Stick Dog raised his paws to signal her to stop.

But it was too late.

Obviously not seeing the glass door and never adjusting her speed, Karen bumped her head right into it. She fell down instantly but popped back up just as quickly. She rubbed her forehead with her right front paw. The look on her face showed her pain, but it indicated sadness and frustration even more. She now knew

it wasn't going to be easy to get back to her friends.

Stick Dog pushed his shoulder into the doorframe as hard as he could a couple of times.

It didn't budge.

Instantly, Karen's face turned from sadness and frustration to panic. On the other side of the glass, Stripes, Mutt, and Poo-Poo were pacing and circling nervously.

Stick Dog gave the doorframe a final shove, but nothing happened. "It's locked," he said, and panted. "We can't get her out this way."

"Oh, yes we can," said Poo-Poo. He took several steps away from the door, lowered his head battering-ram style, and said, "Stand back, everybody."

Stripes and Mutt stepped quickly out of the way. Even Karen, who couldn't hear Poo-Poo but certainly recognized the familiar head-smashing-into-something

stance, stepped back on her side of the glass door.

Stick Dog didn't move. "Stop, Poo-Poo," he said, holding up a front paw, pads toward Poo-Poo. "We can't have you crashing your head through a glass door. That's dangerous."

"What about the wall?" asked Poo-Poo sincerely.

Stick Dog smiled. "Yes. If we can't figure out another way," he answered. "Then you can try breaking through the wall."

Poo-Poo tapped his forehead three times against the patio, then lifted up his head and said, "I'll be ready."

After looking over both her shoulders, Karen came closer and put her front paws up against the glass. Her eyes were pleading. She dropped back to all fours suddenly. And then she was gone.

"Where'd she go?" asked Stripes.

"She ran off," said Stick Dog. A single second later he said, "Quick! Hide! She must have heard the human coming!"

Poo-Poo and Mutt scurried behind the grill and some flowerpots. Stripes ducked behind a big pot with a tomato plant growing in it. Stick Dog dove behind a chair. They could all still see through the glass door. And, sure enough, the big man with the beard came into the room.

He began searching through the laundry
basket.

"He's looking for Karen!" Mutt whispered.

"He's going to find her!" Stripes exclaimed.

"I'm ready, Stick Dog," Poo-Poo declared,

bumping his head against the grill two times. "Just give the word."

"Stay where you are," Stick Dog whispered. He was watching the human's movements closely and with great seriousness. "I'm pretty sure she's not in the basket again. He would have found her by now. She must be hiding somewhere else."

"That's the strangest hat I've ever seen," whispered Poo-Poo. He was staring at a fuzzy strip of material the man had placed on his head.

"It's hollow," observed Mutt.

"Now what's he doing?" Stripes asked from behind the tomato plant. She had already checked the plant for something to eat, but there were no tomatoes. It was too early in the season. "What the heck are those things?"

The bearded man with the strange, fuzzy, hollow hat reached into the pocket of his shorts and pulled out a wire. The wire plugged into a small box on one end, and from the other end ran a long wire with a

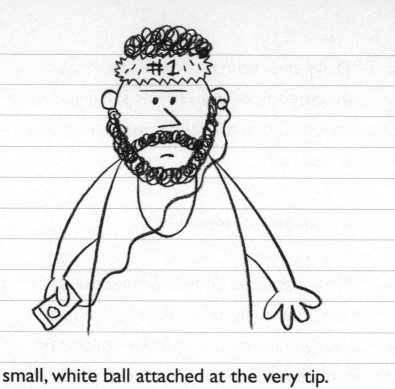

small, white ball attached at the very tip.
He took the small ball and pressed it into
his left ear.

"What the—" Mutt exclaimed.

"What is that thing?" Poo-Poo asked.

"Maybe he's a robot. Or an alien," Stripes

suggested. "That must be his brain antenna receptor."

Poo-Poo nodded. "That explains it. No normal creature would shove something into his ear like that."

"Shh!" Stick Dog said. "He's a human. But I have no idea what he's doing."

"Look! Look!" Stripes said urgently. "Is he dancing?"

The man had spread out his legs very wide and was now leaning forward, trying to touch the floor. He did this several times in a row. He then put his hands on his hips and rotated his abdomen in one direction for a few circles—and then switched directions.

Stick Dog, Stripes, Poo-Poo, and Mutt

stared at the human's peculiar behavior. As
they did, it got even stranger.

His head was rocking rhythmically back
and forth while he
grabbed his right foot
and stretched his right
leg backward. He then
did the exact same thing
to the left side.

"Ouch!" said Stripes,
watching in amazement.
"What kind of freak
would hurt himself like
that?!"

Next, the bearded man balled his hands
into fists and began to swing his arms back

and forth. Simultaneously, he lifted his legs in turn, his knees rising and falling.

The man suddenly stopped, dropped to his stomach, and pushed himself up and

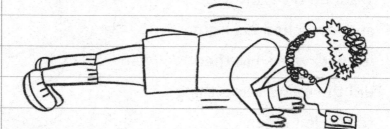

down from the floor with his arms. He did this ten times, still rocking his head in a rhythmic manner.

"Stick Dog?" whispered Mutt. "Can you explain any of this? This guy's scaring me. I mean, really scaring me. I think he's mad at the carpet or something. He's pounding it with his whole body."

"I can't explain it," Stick Dog answered, and shook his head. "Oh no! I think he's coming out. Be ready to run if I say so."

Indeed, the bearded man with the wire in his ear had stood up and walked toward the sliding glass door.

"Should we run?" Poo-Poo asked. "Please say yes. I want to get out of here!"

"No, wait," said Stick Dog. "Hold still. I don't think he's coming out."

The man did not reach toward the handle to slide the door open. Instead, he turned his body sideways and stared blankly at

the glass. He then sucked in his belly and puffed out his chest. He did this several times.

And then he left.

The dogs all looked at each other with shock on their faces. They had never seen such a weird display of actions from a human.

Finally, Mutt asked the question that all of them were thinking. He asked, "What was Mister Beard-O Strange-O doing in there?"

It was quiet for a moment while they tried to figure it out. Then Poo-Poo provided a theory.

"I think I know," he said. There was confidence in his voice, as if the correct answer had suddenly dawned on him—and he was now quite sure of it.

"What?" asked Mutt.

"I've seen birds doing it in the forest," Poo-Poo answered. "It's called a mating dance. He's trying to attract a girlfriend."

"That makes sense," said Mutt.

"Well, of course," said Stripes. "I was just about to think of that myself."

Poo-Poo, now gaining even more confidence from his friends' reactions, continued. "That's why he did it here in front of the glass door. He's hoping a female is looking in. Obviously, there wasn't one around, so he stopped."

Mutt and Stripes nodded and then turned

to Stick Dog. "What do you think, Stick Dog? Do you think all that stuff was a human mating dance?"

"I don't know," answered Stick Dog. He then shook his head vigorously for a couple of seconds. It looked like he was trying to shake the visual memory of the human's behavior out of his mind. When he stopped shaking his head, Stick Dog tilted it ever so slightly to the side. "Wait a minute. Quick! To the screen door at the front of the house! Follow me!"

"Why?" Poo-Poo asked, tensing up and getting ready to run.

"I'll explain when we get there."

They ran along the side of the house to the front. To their good fortune, there was a line of bushes on either side of the front door. The heavy main door was open, but the screen door was closed securely. They hid out of sight between the house and the bushes. Panting and crouching there, Mutt asked Stick Dog, "What's the plan?

Why are we here?"

"This is going to be easy," said Stick Dog, looking at each of them in turn. "That human is getting ready to exercise. He's going to come out any minute and ride a bike or run down the sidewalk. That's what he was doing in there—getting his body ready to move."

"You mean it wasn't a mating dance?" asked Stripes.

"I don't think so," said Stick Dog.

"I'm not so sure, Stick Dog," said Poo-Poo doubtfully. "I think he was trying to get a girlfriend. Let's be honest; that guy looks desperate."

Stick Dog was nodding his head while listening to Poo-Poo. He was also searching under the bush for something. In a few seconds, he had a long stick in his mouth. He dropped it right in front of him and then addressed Poo-Poo.

"You might be right—and I might be wrong, Poo-Poo," said Stick Dog quickly. "He may have been performing a mating dance ritual or he may have been getting ready to run on the sidewalk. Either way, I think he's going to be coming out this door any minute—either to start running or biking. Or to look for a girlfriend."

This was enough to satisfy Poo-Poo. "You're right: either one of us could be correct," he said. "What do we do when he comes out?"

"I know how these doors work," said Stick Dog. "They swing open fast when humans push on them. But they close slowly before slamming shut. We're going to hide right here. When he comes out to run or bike or whatever—"

"Or go hunting for a little lovey-dovey," added Poo-Poo.

"Right, or, umm, what you said," Stick Dog

conceded. "That door will close slowly behind him. He'll be several steps away, and I'll slip this stick into the door before it closes. It won't shut all the way, and we'll be able to push it open and let Karen out."

They crouched down and waited for the bearded human to come to the door.

After three minutes, someone did come.

It wasn't the man with the beard.

Chapter 8

PLUMMETING CLUMSILY

It was Karen.

She stood on her back
paws and put her front
paws up on the door
and pressed her nose to
the screen, stretching it
forward.

Stick Dog saw her first. He ran out from
between the bush and the house. He

spoke urgently. "Get back! I think that human is about to come out! When he does, I'm going to slip this stick into the door. It won't close, and you can escape! Go hide again! Fast!"

By this time, Mutt, Stripes, and Poo-Poo had emerged from the hiding spot too. They were all crowded around the door now.

"I'm so glad you're safe," said Poo-Poo. He was shaking with nervous energy.

"Me too!" said Mutt.

"Did you find anything to eat in there?" asked Stripes.

"Just crumbs," Karen answered casually. "I hid under the kitchen table when I heard him coming earlier. You know, back by the glass door."

Stick Dog was curious. "Why are you so calm? Don't you want to get out of there?"

"Oh, yeah," answered Karen. "This guy's a real nut ball. Did you see all that weird stuff he was doing?"

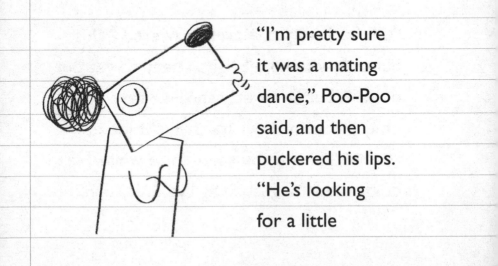

"I'm pretty sure it was a mating dance," Poo-Poo said, and then puckered his lips. "He's looking for a little smooncha-smooncha. If you know what I mean."

Karen nodded her head. "That makes sense, I guess. Even though that's really gross to think about."

Stick Dog tried to get them back on subject. He couldn't understand why Karen was not panicked. "So why are you so calm?"

"Oh, yeah. Right," Karen answered. "This human's whacko, all right. I need to get out of here. But I'm pretty sure we have some time. He went downstairs, and it looks like he's going to be there for a while. He's doing the strangest thing I've ever seen."

"Stranger than before?" asked Stripes.

Karen nodded. "He went down some steps and didn't come up. And he was making some weird noises. So I went to have a look. I went down a couple of steps and took a peek."

"What did you see?" asked Mutt.

"What was he doing?" Poo-Poo asked.

"What kind of crumbs were there under the kitchen table?" asked Stripes.

"Nothing very good. Crackers and stale bread, I think," Karen answered.

Stick Dog shook his head a little. They had to get Karen out of there. And even if they did have more time to do so than he thought, it didn't change the fact that he had quickly gone from pretty hungry to almost starving. His stomach was growling almost constantly now. And he knew that darn raccoon, Phyllis, was probably getting closer and closer to that frankfurter cart. "Why do you think we have plenty of time?"

"He's doing this odd thing downstairs," said Karen. "He's running."

"Running? Inside?" asked Stripes.

"Running. Inside."

"In a circle?" asked Mutt, tilting his head slightly. "Like when you chase your tail and don't catch it?"

"I caught it once. On January sixteenth. Best day ever," Karen corrected. And then

she said, "No, he's running in a straight line."

"A straight line?! He must be running face-first into the wall over and over," said a wide-eyed Poo-Poo. "I'm starting to like this human."

Karen smiled and shook her head. "No, no.

He's on this machine that has its own floor, sort of. The floor goes around and around. He runs but doesn't move."

Stripes, Poo-Poo, and Mutt all had confused expressions on their faces, trying to picture what Karen was describing. They turned toward Stick Dog to see if he could explain it. He usually could.

"He runs but doesn't go anywhere. On purpose," Stick Dog said, as much to himself as to the others. "What kind of creature would do that? It's ridiculous."

It was then that they felt a strong breeze. It flapped the sheets and clothes that were drying on the line. And, more important, it blew the aromas from the frankfurter cart in their direction. They all lifted their noses and sniffed at the meaty scent.

"Okay," Stick Dog said. "Who cares? This human likes to shove little things in his ears, he moves his body in strange ways, and he's running without going anywhere. It doesn't matter. He can be as strange as he wants to be. That's his business, not ours. Our business is getting Karen out of this house and then snatching those frankfurters."

With the help of the frankfurter smells drifting past, it was easy for them all to refocus on their mission.

"Now, if he's not going to be coming through this door anytime soon, how are we going to get you out of there?" asked Stick Dog. "There has to be a way."

"There is," said Karen. "There's a window open at the back of the house. I found it when I was looking around. I'm just going to hop out."

"Really?" Stick Dog said, clearly surprised. "Why didn't you hop out before?"

"Well, I wanted to get all of the crumbs I could," Karen admitted. "And then I thought I heard you guys out here. I didn't want you to worry."

"There's really an open window?" asked Stick Dog.

"Really."

"Well, how about that?" said Stick Dog, smiling. "Finally, an easy solution. No elaborate plans or sneaking around. Great. We'll meet you in the back then."

Karen winked and pointed a paw at Stick Dog, pressing it against the screen. "You betcha."

They stalked away from the front door, careful to stay out of the view of Peter, the frankfurter man. They scurried on their bellies to stay low and out of sight.

They stopped once about halfway. Another breeze had lifted one of the sheets, and they paused to look at the frankfurter cart and sniff that meaty scent drifting on the wind. When they looked, however, they saw something else.

Phyllis was now positioned in a sycamore tree—much closer to Peter and the cart. And that wasn't the worst of it.

Now she had three other raccoons with her. There were a total of four puffy, ringed tails hanging out of the leaves of that big sycamore tree.

They all noticed at once.

"Oh no!" said Stripes.

"She's got help!" whispered Mutt.

"She's assembled an
entire Frankfurter Assault
Squadron!" Poo-Poo
exclaimed.

"Shh," whispered Stick
Dog. He didn't like the
looks of this either, but the frankfurters
were no longer their top priority. "We
have to get Karen first. She should be back
there by now."

They scurried the rest of the way to the
patio.

"Where's Karen?" asked Stick Dog, looking
around when they arrived. "I thought she'd
be here by now."

"Here I am," Karen called. She was leaning out of a window on the second floor of the house. "I took one last look for crumbs. Sorry to keep you waiting. Clear out a spot for me! I don't want to land on anyone!"

She then ducked back inside.

"Karen! No!" yelled Stick Dog. "No! Don't jump!"

She came back to the window, and Stick Dog exhaled.

"Why not?" asked Karen calmly. "You want me to check out the kitchen for scraps? I'm pretty sure there's nothing else there. But I guess I might have missed something."

Stick Dog dropped his head and looked at the ground for a minute. Then he came closer to the house—and closer to Karen. He looked up at her from the lawn. "You can't jump from that high up. You'll break every bone in your body," he sighed. "When you said you found an open window and were going to jump out, I just assumed it was on the first floor."

Stripes came up to Stick Dog then and put a paw on his shoulder. "You really shouldn't make assumptions, Stick Dog," she said. "It can totally mess things up. It's like how I *assumed* you could fly a helicopter. That assumption messed up the whole plan.

Otherwise, we'd be feasting on frankfurters by now. You should have learned from that."

Stick Dog gently removed Stripes's paw from his shoulder. "You're right," Stick Dog whispered. "I'll try to keep that in mind, Stripes. Thanks."

"Glad to help," Stripes replied.

Stick Dog looked at Karen high up in the second-floor window. "Stay there," he said. "I'll be right back."

"Okay," Karen called.

"You guys stay here too," he said to Mutt, Stripes, and Poo-Poo. In a quieter voice that only they could hear, he said, "Don't let her jump. This will just take a minute."

Stick Dog ran to the corner of the house and slowly leaned his head out to look at Peter, the frankfurter man. "Come on, come on," Stick Dog whispered. "Do something."

He did.

Peter turned around, leaned down, and began to tie his shoe.

Stick Dog's eyes opened wide. "I don't believe it," he said.

He ran as fast as he
could to the laundry
line and ripped
down one of the
two sheets drying
there. Without even
glancing back, he
raced back to the
corner of the house
with the sheet clenched in his jaws. Once
he turned the corner, he stopped and
dragged the sheet the rest of the way
behind the house. He took one look at
Peter and smiled.

Peter was just now standing back up from
tying his shoe.

Stick Dog took the sheet to the lawn

beneath the window.

"Help me spread this out," he said.

They all worked to spread the sheet out
while Karen watched from above.

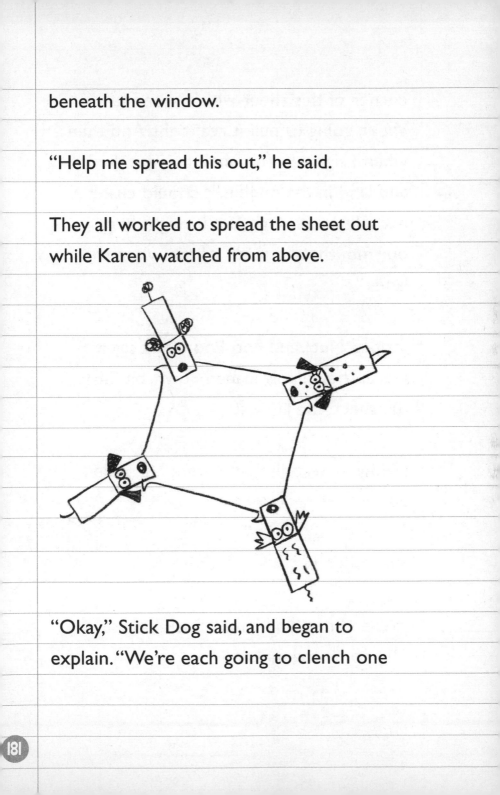

"Okay," Stick Dog said, and began to
explain. "We're each going to clench one

corner of this sheet with our mouths.
We're going to pull it real tight. And then
when I signal Karen, she's going to jump
and land in the middle. It should cushion
her fall just enough. But it might hurt
our mouths and teeth a little when she
lands."

Stripes, Mutt, and Poo-Poo didn't say a
word. They simply leaned down, bit into
the sheet, and lifted it.

"Did you hear all that, Karen?" he called
up.

She nodded.

"When I nod, you jump," Stick Dog said.
"Try to hit the middle."

She nodded again.

And Stick Dog picked up his corner of the sheet.

Okay, we have to stop here for a minute. I'm sorry; I know it's kind of an important part of the story, but I need to make something clear here.

You know not to go jumping out of windows, right? I mean, I don't have to say that, right? It's dangerous—even if you have four friends holding a sheet real tight under the window. You're way too heavy for the sheet to stop you. Heck, I doubt if it would even slow you down.

So no jumping out windows, okay?

Good. Now back we go.

With clear determination on his face and in his eyes, Stick Dog looked in succession at Mutt, Poo-Poo, and Stripes. Each of them had a solid grip on the sheet and were scooting backward to pull it tight. When it was as taut as it could be, Stick Dog raised his eyes to Karen.

He nodded his head.

And Karen jumped.

Do you know what the word "majestic" means? It means awe-inspiring. The Grand Canyon or Niagara Falls would be considered majestic, for instance. The Golden Gate Bridge in San Francisco is considered a majestic work of architecture. When referring to movement, it means really beautiful and graceful. An eagle soaring through the sky is majestic.

When Karen jumped from that window, she was not majestic. There was nothing beautiful or graceful about it. First, she caught one of her back paws on the windowsill, which made her start tumbling immediately. And she wasn't quite falling. It was more like plummeting. In fact, I think the best way to describe her descent would be this: she plummeted clumsily.

But here's something really important: while her fall was not majestic, her aim was perfect.

She landed on her back right in the middle of that sheet. Stick Dog, Stripes, Mutt,

and Poo-Poo clenched the material with
all their strength. They braced themselves
with their front legs as hard as they could,
but they were still pulled inward with
Karen's impact on the sheet.

It sagged rapidly with her weight, and
everyone pulled as hard as they could. The
sheet brushed against the green blades
of grass beneath and then rose again,
bouncing Karen safely to the side, where
she landed right-side up on the patio.

Then she bowed.

"Thanks, everybody," she said as the other
four dropped the sheet and stretched
their mouths and jaws. Then she sniffed at
the air. And Stripes, Poo-Poo, and Mutt did

too. Karen said, "Those frankfurters smell delicious, don't they?"

Stick Dog smiled and said, "Let's go get them."

Chapter 9

STACKIFYING

With Karen safely rescued from the bearded man's house, the possibility of eating a whole bunch of those delicious-smelling frankfurters was now at the forefront of all of their minds. From the corner of the house, the five dogs waited and waited for Peter to turn his head in the other direction so they could sprint to the remaining sheet on the line and hide behind it.

"I'm not going alone this time," Karen declared. "No way."

"We'll all go together," Stick Dog agreed. "We just have to wait for Peter to turn the other way."

Do you like waiting? Not me. In fact, I think waiting is one of the worst things in the entire world. If I have to wait for something—like in the grocery line or at the doctor's office or to fall asleep at night when I'm really, really NOT TIRED and THERE IS NO REASON IN THE WORLD WHY I SHOULD HAVE TO

GO TO BED SO EARLY AND LIFE IS SO
INCREDIBLY UNFAIR THAT I COULD
JUST SCREAM!—then I try to occupy
my mind with something else. Like
maybe I'll count to 1,056 by sixes, or try
to name twenty-two flavors of ice cream.

Do you know what my favorite flavor is?
You're not going to believe this. It's vanilla.
The most boring flavor of all. Now, that
doesn't mean I'm boring, okay? In fact, I can
prove how NOT BORING I am. Yesterday I

fell *up* the stairs. That's right: UP. Anybody can fall *down* the stairs, but not too many can fall up like me. That is definitely not boring.

It's painful. It's a little embarrassing. But it's not boring.

Anyway, I don't like waiting. Yuck. You know the worst waiting thing of all time? Waiting to get to a really exciting conclusion of a story. Yeah, that's terrible, all right.

Oh. Umm, yeah.

Back to the story.

Finally, Peter turned his head. And when he did, all five dogs sprinted to where the

laundry was hanging from the clothesline
in the yard of the blue house. They skidded
to a stop behind the sheet, where they
couldn't be seen.

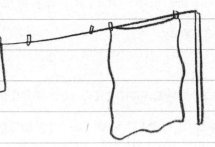

But there was a problem.

The sheet was hanging almost all the way to the ground. They couldn't see Peter from under it. And it was flapping in the wind just enough that they might be seen along either side of it if they tried to peek out that way.

"How are we going to tell if he's turned his head again so we can go grab the frankfurters?" asked Mutt.

It was a very good question—and Stick Dog did not have an immediate answer.

But Poo-Poo did. First, he explained their situation.

"Look," he said, "we can't see under this big cloth thing because it's hanging down

to the ground. And we can't see around
either side because the wind is flapping it
all over the place and we're going to get
spotted. There's only one thing to do. We
have to look over it."

"Great idea," said Karen. Then, with all
her mighty dachshund strength, she began
jumping up and down to try to see over
the top of the sheet. There was, of course,
only one problem. Karen could only jump
several inches off the ground. She stopped

after a few more attempts, realizing that it was absolutely useless. "But how?"

"We climb on top of each other until we can see over the top!" said Mutt.

All the dogs nodded their heads with great enthusiasm at hearing this suggestion.

Except for Stick Dog. "No way," was all he said.

"Why not?" asked Poo-Poo.

"We'll never keep our balance. We'll fall down all over the place and break our legs and tails. It will be a mess. A total mess."

"Oh," said Stripes, sort of quietly and knowingly. "I see what's going on here."

"What?" sighed Stick Dog. His stomach was beginning to hurt a little. He wanted to taste one of those frankfurters. "What do you think is going on here?"

"I think that you don't like this idea because it's not *your* idea," said Stripes. "We all went along with your idea about running over here and hiding behind this big, square, flappy, soft whatchamacallit. But now that *we* have an idea or two, *you* become the Mister-Always-Says-'No'-to-Everything-He-Ever-Hears Man!"

"That's not . . . ," Stick Dog began, but he realized he was too late. All the other dogs were nodding along with Stripes.

"Yeah, come on, Stick Dog," said Mutt. "We all went along with your plan—now you can go along with ours."

"Yeah, come on!" said Karen and Poo-Poo.

Stick Dog wanted those frankfurters. He wanted them badly. Even if it meant four dogs were going to be falling all over him and breaking his legs and his tail. "Oh, all right."

"Hoo-ray!" the other four dogs exclaimed.

And with that, they started climbing up

all over each other. There was not much
organization or thought behind the process.
And Stick Dog had given up trying to
convince them of the proper way to do
it—with the biggest dog at the bottom and
the smallest on the top. Instead, they just
started bashing together and climbing and
falling and climbing and falling and climbing
and falling. They got all tangled up and then

untangled themselves and then got all tangled up again.

One time, Stripes asked, "Whose tail is in my mouth?"

Stick Dog looked back over his shoulder to look at Stripes and see whose tail was in her mouth. When he saw the answer, he said, "It's yours, Stripes. It's your own tail."

"It is not."

"Yes, it is."

"I would know my own tail, wouldn't I?"

"You would think so, yes."

"So, then it's not my tail."

"Try this," suggested Poo-Poo, overhearing the conversation. "Bite down a little bit."

"Okay," said Stripes, and she bit down. She then yelped and winced at the pain in her own tail and quickly knocked down the entire stack of dogs again.

This is kind of an example of how things

went for about ten minutes or so. After much strenuous effort, the dogs finally got stacked up. And, thankfully, Karen was on top. She was the smallest, and it worked out nicely that way.

So now it was time for Karen to take a peek over the top of the sheet—and see when Peter, the frankfurter man, turned his head in the other direction. When he did, they could de-stackify themselves, run to the cart, grab the frankfurters, and hightail it back to Stick Dog's pipe for the feast.

One problem.

It didn't work out that way.
Instead, here's what happened.

Karen raised her head ever so slightly over the top of that sheet. When she did, she could see what Peter, the frankfurter man, was up to. And do you know what he was up to?

Nothing.

He was just standing there at his frankfurter cart. He was looking around a little bit, sometimes away from the sheet the dogs were hiding behind, sometimes toward it, but never directly at it. He never turned all the way around. He leaned down to make sure his shoe was still tied. Then he double-knotted both of his shoelaces. He rang the bell on the cart once.

Another time, he kicked a little pebble next to a wheel of his cart. A minute later, he rearranged the ketchup and mustard and salt and pepper, putting them in order from tallest to shortest—ketchup being the tallest. Then he rearranged them from skinniest to plumpest—ketchup being the skinniest.

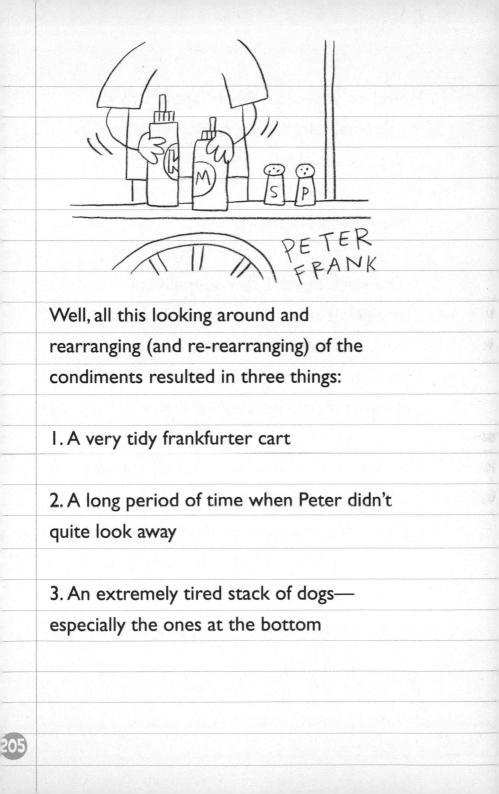

Well, all this looking around and rearranging (and re-rearranging) of the condiments resulted in three things:

1. A very tidy frankfurter cart

2. A long period of time when Peter didn't quite look away

3. An extremely tired stack of dogs— especially the ones at the bottom

And do you know what happens to an extremely tired stack of dogs—especially the ones at the bottom?

Here's what happens:

The stack doesn't stay so solid and straight. It starts to wobble a little. It bends a little bit left. Then it bends a little bit right. It sways a little bit forward. Then it sways a little bit backward. And do you know what happens when more time passes and the dogs—especially the ones at the bottom—begin to get even more tired? Well, that's when the swaying and the tilting start to get even worse.

And that's exactly what happened.

"Hold still down there!" Karen said.

"I'm—uhh—trying," said Poo-Poo. "Hasn't he looked away yet?"

"No, not yet," said Karen. "He's moving the mustard again."

Stick Dog called up to the top of the stack from his position at the bottom, "What about Phyllis?"

"Yeah," Mutt added, wanting to know too. "What about the Frankfurter Assault Squadron? Where are they?"

"They're in a maple tree," Karen observed. "It's only one tree away from the cart. In another minute or two, the Frankfurter Assault Squadron is going to be in the next tree—the one with the branches hanging over the cart. They'll be able to drop down to grab everything!"

Coupled with how tired they were becoming, this news made them all feel very discouraged.

"What about now? Has Peter moved yet?" asked Mutt. "My back's killing me."

"Not as much as my tail," said Stripes.

"That's because you bit yourself," said Poo-Poo.

"Did not."

"Yes, you did. We all saw it. Right, Stick Dog?"

"Shh!" answered Stick Dog with a groan. "I just have to get those frankfurters. I'm so hungry. Is he looking away yet?"

The four other dogs gathered all their strength, inhaled deeply, and concentrated on holding still and keeping the stack steady. They desperately hoped that Karen would answer positively.

Karen peeked at Peter again. He was moving all the condiments back to their original positions. "Nope," was all she said.

At this answer, the stack of dogs began tilting and swaying worse than ever before. It was like all the concentrating energy they used waiting for that final answer from Karen had sapped their remaining strength and stamina. And when they were disappointed with Karen's answer and Peter had not yet turned away, their remaining energy just evaporated. It was inevitable—the stack was going to fall.

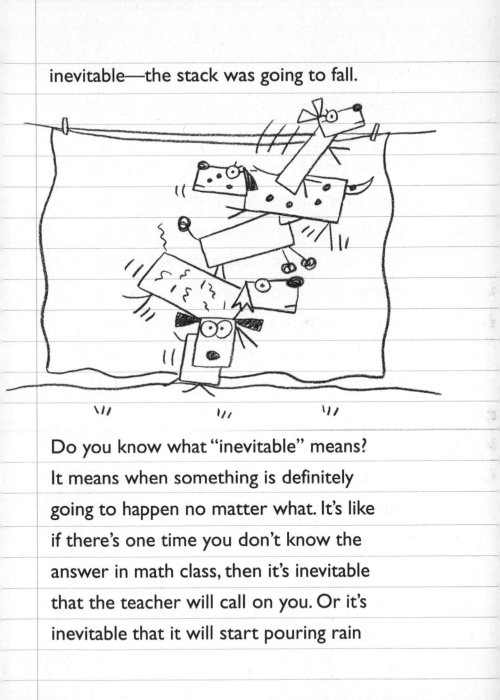

Do you know what "inevitable" means?
It means when something is definitely
going to happen no matter what. It's like
if there's one time you don't know the
answer in math class, then it's inevitable
that the teacher will call on you. Or it's
inevitable that it will start pouring rain

when you're only one block from your house.

Anyway, it was inevitable that the stack of dogs was going to fall. It leaned right, and they all shifted their weight to the left. Then it leaned left, and they shifted all their weight to the right. They regained an even balance just for a second, then the whole stack began to lean backward. And to correct that, they all began to lean forward.

But this time they leaned too far forward. And when they did, three things happened:

1. Karen snagged her nose on the top edge of the sheet.

2. The laundry sheet itself came unhooked from the line.

3. Stick Dog did everything he could to keep the stack on top of him. He really wanted those frankfurters, and he started to stagger forward with the four dogs moving, jiggling, wiggling, swaying, and stumbling on top of him.

Now, from the back, it looked like five dogs piled on top of each other all tangled up in a sheet, stumbling all over the place.

But that was only from the back.

From the front, it looked very different. Very, very different. How different? How about if we just let Peter, the frankfurter man, describe it for us?

"GHOST!"

Peter took one look at that giant white sheet stumbling and bumbling toward him and ran like he never ran before. Now, you might think that somebody like Peter, who has probably had more than a few frankfurters in his day, might be a little slow.

You would be wrong.

When he saw that ghostly creature coming at him, Peter ran like the wind. Like a hurricane wind. Like a hurricane wind combined with a tornado. Like a hurricane wind combined with a tornado that is being chased by a ghost.

That's how fast he ran.

By the time the dogs had stumbled and fallen over to the frankfurter cart, Peter was not even in sight. And by the time they had untangled themselves from the sheet, those five dogs had stopped worrying about Peter altogether. They knew he was long gone—and probably was not coming back for a very long time.

Poo-Poo, Stripes, Mutt, and Karen snatched all the frankfurters they could carry and sprinted off to the safety and comfort of Stick Dog's empty pipe. Stick Dog looked up into the maple tree just a few feet away from the cart. The four raccoons were situated on a lower branch. They looked hungry—and disappointed.

Stick Dog reached into the cart and grabbed a bunch of frankfurters. He carried them to the maple tree and

dropped them gently at the base of the
trunk.

Returning to the cart, he snatched another

bunch of frankfurters and raced to catch
up with Mutt, Karen, Stripes, and Poo-Poo.

When they all reached Stick Dog's pipe,
they started to eat the frankfurters. And
they laughed and laughed at how they had
scared Peter, the frankfurter man, away.
And they congratulated themselves on

defeating the Frankfurter Assault Squadron.
Between laughs and congratulations, they
took more frankfurter bites.

And those frankfurters, oh, those
frankfurters.

They tasted so good.

And Stick Dog's stomach was finally—and
happily—silent.

QUIET

The End.

Turn the page for
a sneak peek at
the next Stick Dog
adventure!

Stick Dog slowly straightened his body and dropped the cardboard circle to the ground. "You have to taste that thing," he whispered. "I can't believe I'm saying this—but I think it tastes even better than hamburgers and frankfurters."

"That's impossible," muttered Karen, but she had learned a long time ago to trust Stick Dog when it came to the subject of food. All four dogs began licking the cardboard. And Stick Dog dropped his head for another taste too.

Stripes lifted her head momentarily and asked, "What is this red, sticky stuff?"

"Here, let me see," said Poo-Poo, and he nudged his nose into a red splotch of stuff that was smeared across one section of the cardboard. He sniffed it, licked it, and then bit off a little piece and swirled it around in his mouth a little. He lifted his nose in the air just a bit and then declared with great authority, "That red sticky stuff is delicious, no doubt. It has hints of salt and spice, and a fine clean finish on the back of my palate. It evokes memories of tomato, green pepper, onion, and finely ground pepper."

Coming in Fall 2014

Tom Watson lives in Chicago with his wife, daughter, and son. He also has a dog, as you could probably guess. The dog is a Labrador-Newfoundland mix. Tom says he looks like a Labrador with a bad perm. He wanted to name the dog "Put Your Shirt On" (please don't ask why), but he was outvoted by his family. The dog's name is Shadow. Early in his career Tom worked in politics, including a stint as the chief speechwriter for the governor of Ohio. This experience helped him develop the unique, storytelling narrative style of the Stick Dog books. More important, Tom's time in politics made him realize a very important thing: Kids are way smarter than adults. And it's a lot more fun and rewarding to write stories for them than to write speeches for grown-ups.

For exclusive information on your favorite authors and artists, visit www.authortracker.com.